Patch learns to bark

by Saviour Pirotta

Illustrated by Gill Guile

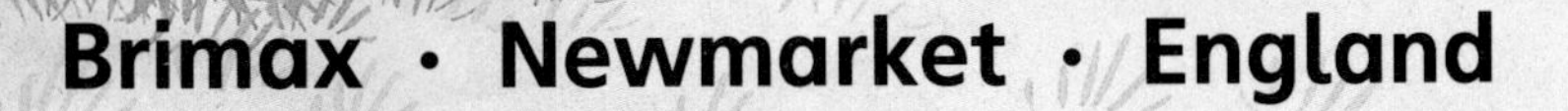
Brimax · Newmarket · England

Patch the Puppy lives with his mother, brothers and sisters on Buttercup Farm. Patch can eat his dinner without spilling any. He can wash behind his ears. But there is one thing Patch cannot do. He cannot bark.

"Do not worry," says Mother Dog. "You will learn to bark like the rest of us."
The other puppies are not so kind. "Patch cannot bark," they laugh. "He can only whimper!"

Patch is so upset that he decides to hide until he has learned how to bark. He does not like his brothers and sisters laughing at him.
He creeps over to the barn and sits behind the hay.
There he tries to bark.

“Goodness me!” says Cassie
Calf who lives in the barn.
“What are you doing there,
Patch?”
“I am learning to bark,”
says Patch unhappily.
“I wish I could help you,”
says Cassie. “I can only moo.”
“Never mind,” says Patch.
He creeps away to find
somewhere else to hide.

Patch does not want anyone else to listen while he tries to bark. At last he finds a dark corner in the hen run. When the chicks hear Patch they say to their mother, "Is there a ghost in the run?" "No!" says Mother Hen. "It is only Patch trying to bark."

“Can you help him, Mother?”
ask the chicks.
“I am afraid not,” says
Mother Hen. “I can only
cluck.”
Patch tiptoes out of the run
and goes to the pig-pen.

When the piglets see Patch they all say, “What are you doing in our pig-pen?”
“I am teaching myself to bark,” says Patch.
“Can we help Patch to bark?” the piglets ask their mother.
“I am afraid not,” says Mother Pig. “We can only grunt.”
Patch goes to the stable.

“What can I do for you?”
asks Dolly Donkey.
“I am teaching myself to
bark,” says Patch.
“I would help you if I could,”
says Dolly. “I can only bray.
You will find your bark sooner
or later.”
“I have tried very hard and
I still cannot bark,” says
Patch.

“I have an idea,” says Dolly. “Why not go and practice in the cellar? You might find your bark there,” she says. Patch leaves the stable and goes to the cellar. The door is wide open.

Patch goes down the stairs very carefully. He sees a chest lying open at the bottom of the stairs. Patch is very curious. He creeps closer and closer to the chest . . .

Suddenly a frog leaps out and lands on Patch's nose! "Woof! Woof!" barks Patch in surprise. "Woof! Woof!" He is so scared he runs back up the stairs. He runs all the way home to his mother, barking as he goes.

"Woof! Woof!" barks Patch as he passes Dolly Donkey in her stable.
"Woof! Woof!" barks Patch as he passes the piglets in their pig-pen.
"Woof! Woof!" barks Patch as he passes the chicks in their run.
"Woof! Woof!" barks Patch as he passes Cassie Calf in her barn.

"Is that you, Patch?" calls
Mother Dog.
"Woof! Woof!" barks Patch.
"I can bark! Something
frightened me in the cellar
and now I can bark!"
Patch's brothers and sisters
crowd round him.
"I am very proud of you,
Patch," says Mother Dog.
"Woof! Woof!" barks Patch
happily.

Say these words again

lives
learn
creeps
hide
corner
afraid
sooner

behind
laugh
somewhere
anyone
trying
teaching
curious